Daniel, the Long-Eared Christmas Donkey

The Best Gift of All

ISBN 978-1-64515-542-3 (paperback)
ISBN 978-1-64515-543-0 (digital)

Christian Faith Publishing, Inc.
832 Park Avenue
Meadville, PA 16335
www.christianfaithpublishing.com

Printed in the United States of America

Daniel, the Long-Eared Christmas Donkey

The Best Gift of All

E.T. Cliff

Hi, my name is Dan, I'm five years old. I'm a miniature donkey. That means I'm much smaller than a normal-sized donkey. I also have very long ears which has made the older and much larger donkeys make fun of me ever since I can remember. So I just go and play all by myself. Here comes one bully right now!

"Hey, runt!" brayed Donny. "I'll bet that you can't go anywhere without tripping over those long ears of yours!"

"Yeah!" the older donkeys brayed together.

I just hung my head low and quietly walked away. "Wait until I'm older. I'll show them! Just because I'm smaller doesn't mean that they are better than me!" I mumbled under my breath.

"You'll never amount to anything!" the older donkeys brayed loudly.

Then one day, while I was waiting for my master to bring me my favorite lunch of oats, corn, and carrots, a man came by, pointed to me, and spoke to my master.

"Sir, I would like to buy your miniature donkey over there. I need him for my pregnant wife to ride to Bethlehem."

"Sir," my master pointed out, "if you need a donkey to help you on your journey, I suggest that you buy one of my stronger larger donkeys who can travel long and far."

"Thank you, but no," said the man. "I've already made up my mind. I would like to buy your smallest one. He'll be just perfect."

From that day forward, I belonged to the man and his wife. My parents told me that they were very special people who were going to help God. I guess that I'm about to find out just how special they are.

When we arrived at their home, I heard the man's wife calling.

"Joseph! I'm glad that you made it home safely! I've missed you so much! Go into the house, eat your supper, and get some rest."

"Not yet, Mary, not until I've introduced you to Daniel. He's going to help you get to Bethlehem so you can have your baby."

"Oh, Joseph, he's so adorable! And look at his long ears, they make him look even cuter! I'll be with you as soon as I show Daniel his new home," said Mary.

Inside the barn, it looked like heaven on earth! By the window, there were *two* bags full of fresh corn, oats, and carrots. It sure smelled delicious! I was so hungry!

Underneath the window was a large trough full of fresh cold water. It sure looked refreshing! I was so thirsty! In the stall, there was new fresh smelling hay. And over the stall door was a handmade fleece blanket.

Then Mary sat on a wooden stool beside me. As she began brushing my ears, she said, "Oh Daniel, your ears are so soft and silky. I could brush them all day and never get tired!"

When she was done, she led me inside the stall and covered me with the fleece blanket. It felt so soft and warm on my tired body that I lay down to rest on the nice new fresh-smelling hay.

Before she left, the last words I heard her whisper were, "Daniel, I'm so looking forward to our journey to Bethlehem together."

After she left, I fell right to sleep. My last thought was I have never felt so at peace in all my life. Before I realized it, it was morning already.

"Good morning, wake up, sleepyhead!" said Mary. "Time to eat your breakfast. We have a long journey ahead of us, and you are going to need all of your strength."

Once everything was packed, we started on our long journey to Bethlehem. When we arrived, we traveled everywhere in the city. But there was no room for my mistress to have her baby.

The last innkeeper that we saw told my master, "Sir, there's a stable just across town where your wife can find shelter to have her baby."

"Thank you," said Joseph.

When we arrived at the stable, I watched the animals that lived there. The cows were eating straw out of the manger. Rams were guarding the entrance. And two turtledoves cuddled with each other high in the rafters. It was warm outside, and friendly inside.

"Hello," I brayed cautiously to the calf.

"Hi!" mooed the calf. "My name is Aaron. What's your name?"

"My name is Dan," I brayed.

"Come, I'd like you to meet my friend Sue, the ewe," mooed Aaron.

"Hey, Dan, I'm so glad to meet you. I hope that we can all be friends," baaed Sue.

"Welcome to Bethlehem!" they both said in unison. "Where did you come from?"

"I came from a village in Nazareth so my mistress could have her baby," I brayed.

"Wow!" baaed Sue. "That's a long way from here! How did you get here?"

"We had to follow this huge star that was big and bright. It had a long tail that stopped here for some strange reason," I brayed.

"Can we see the star?" baaed Sue.

"Just look outside and you can see it for yourself," I brayed.

After I told them about the star, they scurried to the door of the stable and looked outside. "That's really pretty!" baaed Sue.

"Yeah, that's really cool!" mooed Aaron.

I brayed, "Besides, what's so special about this baby anyway? Aren't babies all the same?"

"Well," baaed Sue, "My dad told me that there was going to be a special baby born. It's supposed to be a boy, and he's going to save us from our sins. Whatever that means."

"Do you think that this baby could be that special baby?" mooed Aaron.

"I don't know," I brayed. "We'll just have to wait and see."

Suddenly when Mary let out a very loud cry! The stable grew very quiet. When we looked toward the manger. There seemed to be a strange light all around the newborn baby, at the sound of his first cries, the turtledoves lulled him back to sleep.

Cautiously we huddled in to get a closer look. Stretching our necks forward, we each saw that this baby was tiny, friendly, and he was kind.

"Here, little baby, you can have my wool for your blanket so you won't be so cold," baaed Sue.

"Yeah and here, little baby, you can have my manger for a nice soft bed," mooed Aaron.

Suddenly we heard another voice outside the stable. Quickly we scurried outside to see what was happening.

"Come quickly!" baaed Sue. "Look at this! It looks like a big butterfly flying around!"

"It looks like a big bird to me," mooed Aaron.

"I don't know what it is," I brayed. "But I definitely know that it's not a bird or a butterfly!"

"No, kids, it's an angel," explained Sam, the ram.

"Wow!" mooed Aaron. "I've never seen a real angel before!"

"Neither have I!" I brayed.

"Neither have I!" baaed Sue.

"It's the arch angel Gabriel," added Kym, the cow. "Let's listen to what he has to say."

And the Arch angel Gabriel said unto them, "Fear not, for behold, I bring you tidings of great joy, which shall be to all people. For unto you is born this day in the city of David a Saviour, which is Christ the Lord. And this shall be a sign unto you. Ye shall find the babe wrapped in swaddling clothes, lying in a manger." And suddenly there was a multitude of the heavenly host praising God and saying, "Glory to God in the highest, and on earth peace, good will toward men" (Luke 2:10–14, KJV).

Hurrying back inside, we took a second, closer look at the new baby.

"Wow!" baaed Sue. "Do you see what I see?"

"Yeah," mooed Aaron. "I can actually see the glow around the baby."

"Yes," I brayed. "It takes my breath away!"

"Ours too!" agreed all the other animals.

Then Joseph said to us, "I want you all to meet the baby Jesus. He was born to help us learn to be kind to one another."

"Wow! I didn't know that he was the baby Jesus!" mooed Aaron.

"Neither did I," baaed Sue.

"This baby is really special!" I brayed.

We huddled in even closer to admire baby Jesus now.

Sue baaed, "Wow! Baby Jesus is a miracle just like me!"

Aaron mooed, "Cool! Baby Jesus is handsome just like me!"

And I brayed neat, "Baby Jesus is small just like me!"

"You know what I feel in my heart about the baby Jesus?" mooed Aaron. "I feel like he is going to be caring just like me."

"I feel in my heart that the baby Jesus is going to grow up to be helpful just like me," baaed Sue.

"I feel in my heart that the baby Jesus is going to grow up to be kind just like me," I brayed.

Now that we realized that this was the baby Jesus, we all started to feel that each of our gifts was the best. "Well," baaed Sue, with her nose in the air, "I gave the baby Jesus my wool for his blanket. That makes my gift the best gift of all!"

"No way!" mooed Aaron, strutting around the stable. "I gave the baby Jesus my manger for his bed. That makes my gift the best gift of all!"

"You're both wrong! I carried his mother on my back to this stable so he could be born safely. That makes my gift the best gift of all!" I brayed, sticking out my chest.

"Well, you're all wrong! We lulled the baby Jesus to sleep so he wouldn't cry," cooed Chloe and Jesse, flying high above the rafters. "So that makes our gift the best gift of all!"

"Don't argue," whispered Mary. "You all gave the baby Jesus the gifts that he needed. I will always treasure them in my heart."

Suddenly we heard a strange, deep voice speaking from the hole in the roof.

"Always remember, gifts that are given from the heart are treasured most by the receiver."

"Who is that?" mooed Aaron.

"It is I, God, that is speaking to you. Always remember to share what you have because that is most pleasing to me."

"That means that we all gave the baby Jesus the best gift of all," I brayed.

"You're right, Dan, baby Jesus did need a warm blanket," mooed Aaron.

"Yeah, baby Jesus needed a safe ride here also," baaed Sue.

"That's right," cooed Chloe and Jesse. "Baby Jesus needed a place to sleep."

"Sure thing," I brayed. "And the baby Jesus needed soft music to lull him to sleep. Do you know what I was just thinking about?"

"No, what were you thinking about?" baaed Sue.

"The best part of this very special autumn day was that we were the only animals to witness the miracle of baby Jesus's birth."

"You're so right!" agreed all the other animals.

"Well," baaed Sue sadly, hanging her head down low, "I guess now that baby Jesus has been born, it means that you have to go home now."

"Yes," I brayed sadly. "I'm going to miss you all very much!"

"We're all going to miss you too!" mooed Aaron.

"Hey, I just realized something. The whole time I was here, nobody made fun of my height or the size of my ears," I brayed.

"Why would we?" baaed Sue. "We are family, and family doesn't make fun of each other."

While we were talking, I brayed, "Did any of you get a funny feeling inside of your tummy that you just can't explain? I did. Suddenly I felt like there was finally *hope* that the world is a place where no one will make fun of each other anymore."

"Yes," mooed Aaron. "I suddenly felt like there was finally going to be *peace* in the world. Nobody will be fighting with each other anymore."

"Me too," baaed Sue. "Baby Jesus gives me a *joy* in my heart that I've never felt before."

Mary whispered to Joseph, "I've never felt as much *love* around us, like the *love* I felt after Jesus was born."

"I know, Mary," Joseph stated. "*Jesus* is truly the *best gift of all*. He brings *love, joy, hope,* and *peace* to all of our hearts!"

About the Author

E. T. Cliff lives in Waterbury, Connecticut. With her cat, MystiBelle. She is a mother to seven children. She's a communicant of First Congregational Church of Waterbury where she served on the Christian education committee. She is also a graduate of the Institute of Children's Literature in West Redding, Connecticut.

She writes stories for elementary school-age children, using the Bible to guide their journey through their everyday lives.

Her motto is, "God can help even his littlest angels with his love and guidance."

Her inspiration for writing her books is Proverbs 22:6 translated, "We as adults should train up the children in our lives in the way they should go so they won't depart from it as adults."

You can contact her through God's Littlest Angels-Home Facebook and Facebook.com/E.T. Cliff, where she welcomes your comments and topic ideas for your children that you want to see written about.

Together we can help our children grow in a positive light.

CPSIA information can be obtained
at www.ICGtesting.com
Printed in the USA
JSHW020959011119
2200JS00001B/8